I0646570

The day Slime took over the house

Written by Roger Carlson

Illustrated by Elena Bogatireva

This book is dedicated to children everywhere who like to use their imagination with slime.

There was a pretty little girl who lived in a lovely house in a lovely neighborhood. She had an adorable dog named Bella. Bella was her best friend and followed her everywhere. This little girl's name was Mariana, and she enjoyed doing a lot of things.

1

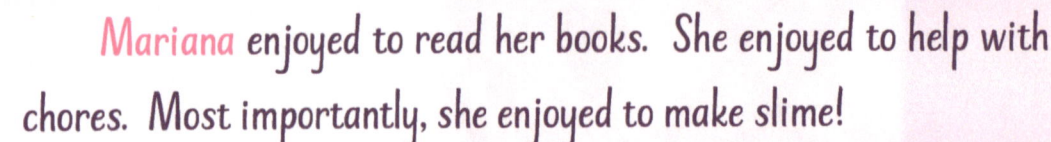

Mariana enjoyed to read her books. She enjoyed to help with chores. Most importantly, she enjoyed to make slime!

Mariana was nine years old. She was fascinated by science. Science class was her favorite. Mariana wanted to be a great scientist when she grew up.

While Mariana was fascinated with Science, her dad liked gardening. "Isn't today such a beautiful Saturday Mariana?" her father, Roger, called out to her. He was busy in the garden trimming some flowers when Mariana scurried out of the house with her dog behind.

4

"Yes, it is," Mariana said. Roger noticed his daughter's hands were stained green, and she had white powder on her face. "Have you been making slime Mariana?" he asked. "Yes daddy, you know how much I love to make slime. It is fun, and it is nice to play with," she smiled.

5

"Good, you can go back and play some more but call me if you need anything." Roger waved at his daughter who ran back into the house with her dog.

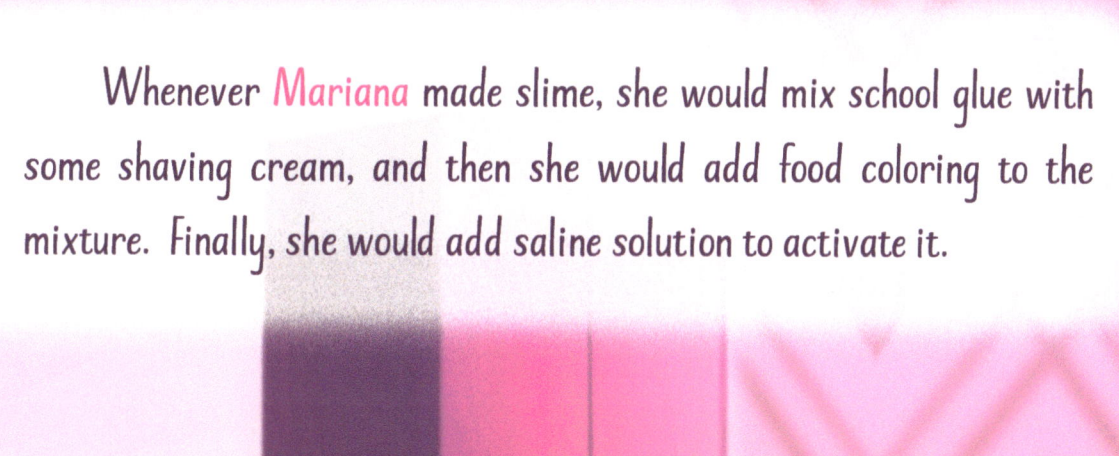

Whenever Mariana made slime, she would mix school glue with some shaving cream, and then she would add food coloring to the mixture. Finally, she would add saline solution to activate it.

7

She did a lot of things with her colored slime. When she was not using letter magnets to spell her name on the slime, she practiced writing lines and drawing shapes on it.

MARIANA

Sometimes, she would hide a button or a bigger object in the slime and ask Bella to find it. To Mariana, everything about slime was fun.

9

"We have made slime in other colors, but we have never made blue slime. What do you think of blue slime Bella?" she asked her dog. Bella barked an answer, " Whoof! Whoof!"

She emptied the bottle of blue dye into the already sticky mixture; everything in the glass bowl turned blue and became gummier. "Wow! Such perfect slime. It is already thick enough to play with. Ready to play?" Bella wagged her tail excitedly and let her tongue out in delight.

"Yeah! Slimy time." Mariana cheered and clapped her hands. She moved near the little table where she kept the glass bowl containing the slime, so she could have a better look at it. This was when Mariana noticed something strange about her bowl of slime.

"Whoof! Whoof!" Bella barked. Bella noticed the strange bubbling in the glass bowl. "Something is not right with this slime; slime never bubbles like that." Mariana frantically said staring at the bowl of bubbling slime.

13

The glass seemed like it was heated by some unknown fire, which made her slime simmer uncontrollably. The bubbling brought forth sloppy and wheezing sounds. Little Mariana was scared. "Maybe I should add more activator to it. Don't you think Bella?"

Bella nodded and rushed towards Mariana's bottle of saline solution that lay at the corner of her little room. She clasped the rope handle in her teeth and brought it to Mariana. "Thank you Bella." Mariana opened the saline activator bottle and emptied all the solution into the bowl. Suddenly, the bubbles vanished, and the slime stopped popping.

"There we are problem solved," Mariana said confidently. She turned her back to the bowl and stared at her dog. Bella had a horrified look on her face. "Is everything alright Bella?" Mariana asked. Bella groaned in a soft voice. It was not all right.

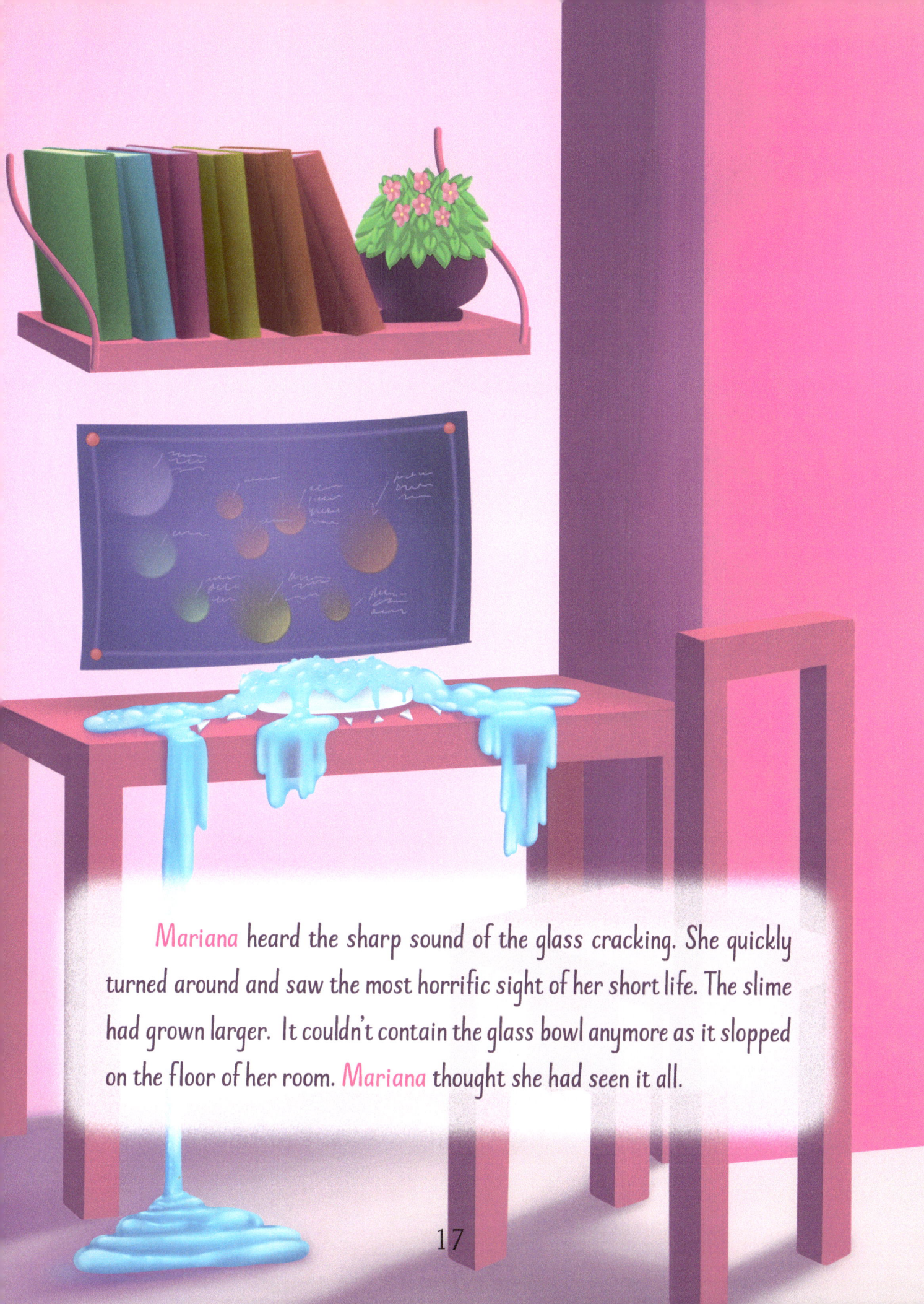

Mariana heard the sharp sound of the glass cracking. She quickly turned around and saw the most horrific sight of her short life. The slime had grown larger. It couldn't contain the glass bowl anymore as it slopped on the floor of her room. Mariana thought she had seen it all.

Before Mariana could say a word, the slime grew and swallowed up her table and then her cupboard. It spread like a fire.

18

"No! You can't do that. That's my dresser!" Mariana screamed as the slime covered her dresser and kept growing. She was scared and angry, "Oh no! What am I going to do? There is slime is everywhere!"

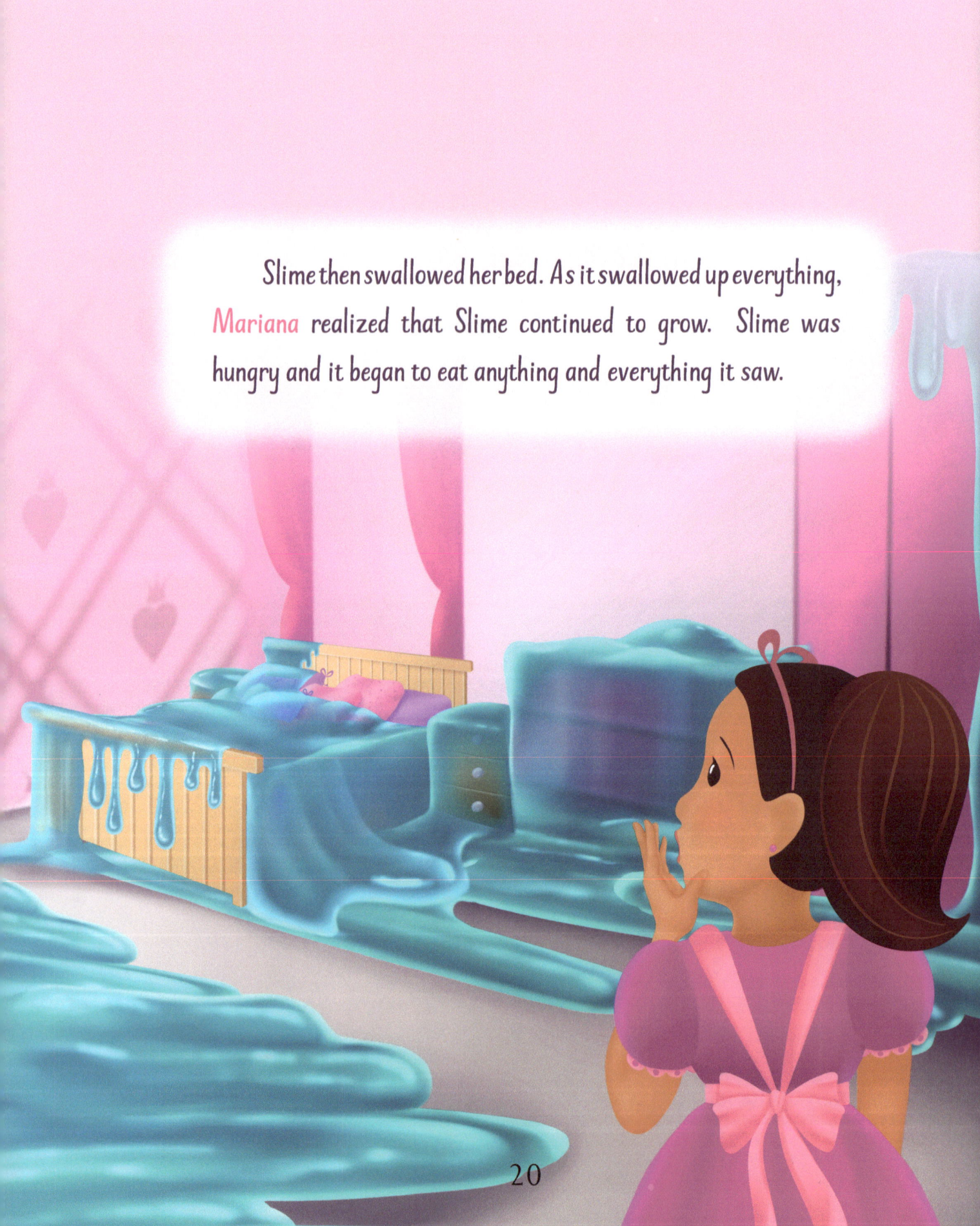

Slime then swallowed her bed. As it swallowed up everything, Mariana realized that Slime continued to grow. Slime was hungry and it began to eat anything and everything it saw.

20

"No!" Mariana yelled. Unknown to her, Slime was attracted to her voice. It began to come towards her. Mariana knew she had to scoop up Bella and run for the door.

"Come on Bella! We need to run!" She hurried
out of the room, Slime chasing after her.

Meanwhile, Dad was still in the garden planting carrots in which they used in making their salad. Suddenly, he heard screaming from the house. He stopped working and listened. At first he thought the screaming was Mariana playing with her dog.

"Daddy!!! Help!!!" He heard her screaming louder this time. Roger knew that something was wrong. He stuck the gardening spade into the black soil and hurried to see what was happening.

Mariana ran as fast as she could. One quick look back sent terror into her little body. Slime was intent on swallowing her.

Tears ran down Mariana's cheeks as she rushed towards the entrance door. If only she could get to the door handle then she thought everything would be alright. She would be able to get out of the house.

Slime was smart. It poured itself on top of the dining room table and chairs and then splashed itself on the door handle. Mariana's escape seemed hopeless.

"No, you can't do that!" Mariana cried as she noticed that Slime had covered the door handle. Slime became angrier at the sound of Mariana's shouting. As a result it decided to pour itself all over the door. Mariana began to weep and Bella just grimaced.

Slime rose higher and higher now engulfing the ceiling fan.

What was Mariana going to do now? Everything was covered with Slime. The walls, floors, tables, chairs and now the ceiling fan were all covered.

"Whoof!" Bella barked near the window.
Mariana realized it was their only escape.

31

"If only we could get there faster than Slime." Mariana whispered to her dog. She loved the idea of opening the window and jumping out. But Slime noticed the girl and the dog were staring at the window, so it quickly plastered a generous portion on the window, making it impossible to be opened.

32

"I think I am going to get sick." Mariana felt nauseous as Slime moved through the kitchen towards her tiny feet. The whole room lay covered in blue except where she was standing with Bella. Her legs were wobbly. Her teeth were chattering. Her lips trembled. There was nowhere for her to run. What was Slime going to do to her and Bella?

Slime crawled towards her, rising first to the level of her knees, which had Mariana in tears. "Please don't eat me. I have never been mean to the slimes. I only love to make you because you are fun to play with." Mariana whispered and closed her eyes. Slime didn't understand. It grew bigger and bigger, swallowing the hem of her dress.

"Daddy! Daddy!" Mariana cried. Why couldn't her father hear her?

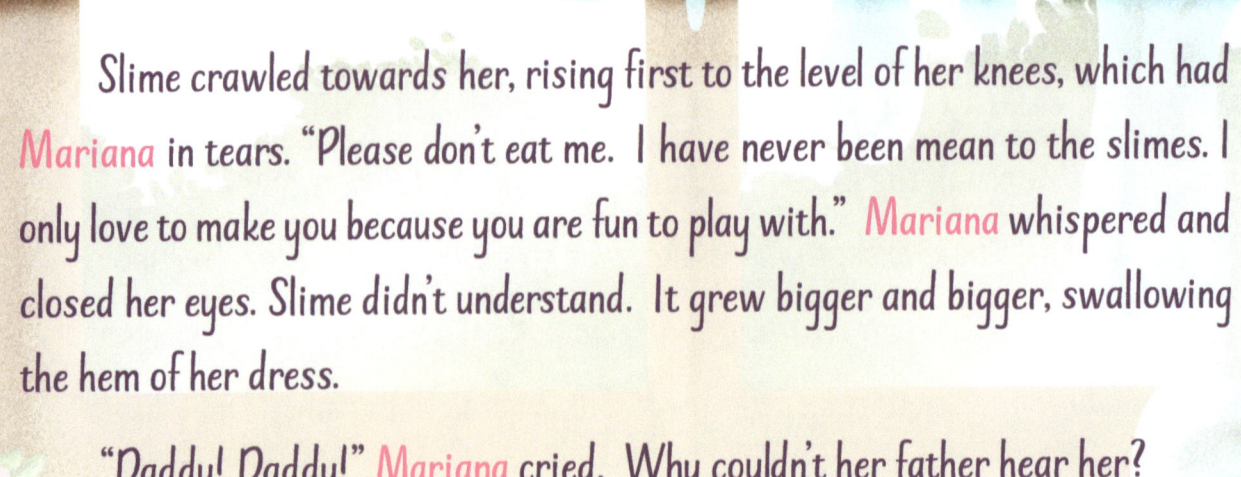

When she thought Slime would swallow her up like everything else in the house, she heard a loud banging.

A bright stream of sunlight seeped into the house, as Roger rushed in.

"What is this?" His eyes grew wide as he stared at the house.

Something happened as Roger opened the door. Slime began to shrink just as quickly as it had grown. Everyone watched in disbelief as Slime shrunk.

37

"What happened here Mariana?" Roger still couldn't understand what caused Slime to shrink so quickly. Was it the fresh air? Was it the pure sunshine? Did the loud bang as he was breaking through the door startle Slime? Did something that Slime touch in the house affect it? They cleaned up what was left of the blue slime throughout the house.

When they finished cleaning, Mariana gave Bella one more hug and said, "This is why we have to treasure the time we have together Bella." They continued to ask themselves questions. Was Slime friendly or was it mean? In the end there were many unanswered questions that day.

The only thing Roger and Mariana know for sure is that they never want that to happen again. Mariana and Roger sat down to read a bed time story.

As they drifted off to sleep Roger had visions of watering his carrots with blue slime.

Mariana dreamed she mixed the most powerful purple slime the world had ever seen.

Bella buried the blue food coloring in the back yard before she settled down to sleep.

Slime on kids and FOLLOW UP

Keep an eye on Mariana Publishing LLC other current and future books.

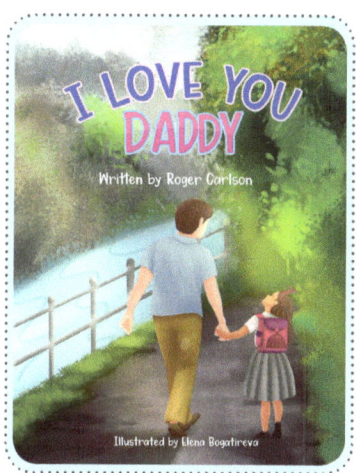

I Love You Daddy

*Mariana Wayback Book-
Washington's Riddles*

*Precious Moments
with Dick and Jane*

*The day Slime took over
the neighborhood*

For more inspirational books visit our web site
www.marianapublishing.com

Find us on:

ABOUT THE AUTHOR

ROGER CARLSON holds a Bachelors degree in Education and an MBA, both from Indiana University. In addition, he has an undergraduate degree in Electrical Engineering Technology from Purdue. During his career, Roger has worked as a math teacher and a mechanical and electrical engineer. Roger is the single dad of an amazing girl.

Roger has cleaned up hundreds of slime messes over the years. There are slime stains in several areas of the house. Roger has actually dreamed about slime on many occasions through the development of the book. Roger would like to offer his editor, Roseann Woodka PhD, a special thanks for her tireless assistance. For more inspirational books visit our web site www.marianapublishing.com

Copyright © 2019 by Mariana Publishing LLC.

All rights reserved, including the right of reproduction in whole or in part in any form.

All rights reserved. This book or any portion thereof may not be reproduced or used in any manner whatsoever without the express written permission of the publisher except for the use of brief excerpts for review purposes.

ISBN: 978-1-64510-010-2 – Hardback IngramSpark

ISBN: 978-1-64510-011-9 – Softback IngramSpark

ISBN: 978-1-64510-012-6 – Softback KDP

ISBN: 978-1-64510-013-3 – EBook KDP

ISBN: 978-1-64510-014-0 – Softback local printer

First Published in 2019

Printed in the USA